PUPPY PLACE

Patches

ELLEN MILES

SCHOLASTIC

For David, Deb, Margaret, and Sophie, in memory of Lucy.

First published in the US by Scholastic Inc., 2007
This edition published in the UK by Scholastic Ltd, 2008
Scholastic Children's Books
An imprint of Scholastic Ltd
Euston House, 24 Eversholt Street
London, NW1 1DB, UK
Registered office: Westfield Road, Southam, Warwickshire, CV47 0RA
SCHOLASTIC and associated logos are trademarks and or registered trademarks of
Scholastic Inc.

Text copyright © Ellen Miles, 2007

The right of Ellen Miles to be identified as the author of this work
has been asserted by her.

10 digit ISBN 1 407 10602 3
13 digit ISBN 978 1407 10602 1

British Library Cataloguing-in-Publication Data.
A CIP catalogue record for this book is available from the British Library

Printed in the UK by CPI Bookmarque Ltd, Croydon,CR0 4TD
Papers used by Scholastic Children's Books are made from wood grown in
sustainable forests.

1 3 5 7 9 10 8 6 4 2

www.scholastic.co.uk/zone

CHapter ONe

"Bored, bored, bored out of my brain. Bored, bored, bored out of my brain. . ." Sammy sang as he bounced a tennis ball against the wall of the garage.

Jack was bored, too. It was a hot Saturday in May, and he and his best friend had nothing to do.

Well, that wasn't exactly true. There was always something to do, if you asked Jack's mum. "Help me clean out the basement," she'd suggest. Or, "Offer to weed Mrs Schneider's garden". Or, "Take Buddy on a long walk".

The first idea was out of the question. Jack reckoned that ninety-nine per cent of the stuff in the basement had been stored there since long before he was born, so he wasn't responsible for it.

As for Mrs Schneider's weeds, he and Sammy had pulled loads of them last weekend to make up for the living room window they'd broken. Not on purpose, of course. How could they help it if the Schneiders' house was *exactly* where left field would be if there were a left field in their imaginary baseball diamond? Anyway, it had almost been worth it. That inside-the-park home run was the best hit of Jack's baseball career so far.

And Buddy? He was the adorable puppy that Jack Peterson and his family had adopted. Jack loved Buddy more than anything. He was the perfect puppy. Buddy had big brown eyes, soft, toast-coloured fur, floppy ears, and a little white heart on his chest. His breath smelled sweet and his tiny baby teeth were so white (and sharp!). He was always happy and always ready for a game or a snuggle.

Buddy was growing up fast. Sometimes Jack still

couldn't believe that Buddy would belong to him *for ever*! The Petersons had been the foster family for lots of puppies, giving each one a safe place to live while they found it the perfect home. But Buddy was different. Buddy had come to stay.

Buddy got lots and lots of attention from everybody in the family. He'd already been on *two* long walks that day, once with Lizzie, Jack's older sister, and once with Jack and Dad and the Bean.

Jack's little brother, the Bean, did have a real name – Adam – but nobody ever called him that. The Bean was two, and the funny thing about him was that he liked to pretend he was a dog. Some people might think that was weird, but the Petersons were used to it. And it was easiest to just play along.

So that morning, when Jack had got out Buddy's red lead, the Bean brought over his green lead, too. He sat up straight and eager while Jack clipped it on to a little green harness Mum had made for him. You could practically imagine the Bean's tail wagging. Dad took hold of the Bean's lead while Jack held Buddy's, and they walked all the way down to the playground and back. The Bean hardly barked at all, so Jack and Dad gave him a chocolate when they got home. Buddy got a dog biscuit.

Now Buddy and the Bean were both inside, taking a nap together on Buddy's red-tartan dog bed. That was the Bean's favourite place to sleep, curled up with Buddy and a stuffed dog toy.

"We could walk Buddy again, I guess," Jack said to Sammy. He knew the puppy was always happy to be taken out. For Buddy, every walk was an adventure.

"Goldie and Rufus would probably like another walk, too." Sammy and his parents lived next door with two golden retrievers, an older one, Rufus, and a puppy, Goldie. Goldie was the first puppy the Petersons ever fostered. "Only. . ."

"Only – *what*?" Jack was suspicious. He had

4

noticed that Sammy had a certain gleam in his eye, the one that meant he had a capital P Plan. And Sammy's Plans often led to trouble.

"Only . . . the dogs might get scared if we go where I think we should go."

Now Jack was curious. "Where's that?"

"To the haunted house." Sammy let the ball bounce away down the driveway. Then he told Jack a story he had heard from an older boy at school. "Harry Bremer says there's a ghost in this house near his, over by the cemetery. He says he hears it moaning all the time. Night time, daytime, it doesn't matter. That ghost is always wailing."

"Has – has he seen it?" Jack did not like to admit that he was afraid of ghosts.

"Not yet. Nobody has. So we'll be the first!"

Suddenly, helping Mum clean out the basement was sounding a lot more interesting. But Jack knew how Sammy was. When he came up with a Plan, he just *had* to follow through. And he expected company.

Half an hour later, Sammy and Jack rode their bikes around a corner near the cemetery and stopped short. It was obvious which house was haunted. It had to be the enormous, rambling grey mansion that looked like it belonged in a scary film.

Jack could tell right away that nobody had lived in that house for a long, long time. Its windows and doors were crooked. Twining vines with poisonous-looking purple flowers crawled all over the falling-down porch. The garden was full of weeds, most of them taller than Jack. And a rusty bicycle lay near the front steps, like someone tossed it down twenty years ago and never came back to pick it up.

Jack swallowed. His mouth felt dry. "I – I don't hear any moaning," he said.

"Me neither." Sammy leaned his bike against the fence and pulled open the creaking gate. "Maybe we have to get closer."

6

Jack wanted to run in the opposite direction, but Sammy was already halfway down the front walk. He couldn't abandon his friend! Jack left his bike next to Sammy's and tiptoed through the gate.

"Dare you to go up on the porch!" Sammy had stopped near the rusty bicycle.

Jack shook his head. "No, thanks." He took a closer look at Sammy. Could his friend be scared, too?

But Sammy just shrugged and started up the rotten wooden stairs. Then, mid-step, he froze. "Do you hear what I hear?"

Jack gulped. He nodded. He heard it, all right. And it sent chills down his spine. The low moaning sound seemed to fill the air around him.

"Where's it *coming* from?" Sammy tilted his head.

"I don't know, but—" Jack was about to say that it must be just about time to go home for lunch, but Sammy interrupted.

7

"Come on! Let's find out."

Jack had no choice but to follow Sammy up on to the porch. The boys cupped their hands and peered into the windows of the dark, empty, tumbledown house.

"Nothing." Sammy sounded disappointed. Jack hoped that meant they could leave. But the moaning didn't stop.

"I think it's coming from the back," Sammy said, after he'd listened for a moment. He led the way around the porch. Jack followed, watching where he put his feet so that he didn't fall through the rotten boards. When Sammy stopped short, Jack almost slammed into him. "Look!" Sammy pointed.

Jack could hardly believe his eyes. The sad moaning sound was not coming from any ghost. It was coming from a dog! A puppy, actually. A little brown puppy that was tied up in the garage next door.

Chapter Two

Sammy stared at Jack.

Jack stared at Sammy.

There was no ghost. There was just a tiny, cute brown puppy, crying and howling for attention.

Ohhhhh, waahhhhh, I'm sooooooo loooooonely! Sooooommmebody pleeeeeease plaaaaaaay with meeeeee!

The puppy threw back his head and howled even louder when he saw Jack and Sammy. How could such a big sound come out of such a little puppy?

"I can't take it!" Sammy put his hands over his ears.

"The poor little guy!" Jack ran right down the porch stairs and into the next-door neighbour's garden. He cut across the driveway and knelt by the puppy. The tiny dog looked up at him with soft brown eyes. When he held up one little paw, Jack felt his heart melt. What was this cute little guy doing out here all by himself?

"Jack! What are you *up* to?" Sammy was still standing on the porch.

"He needs help!" The puppy was tied to a long rope. And the rope was tangled around a bicycle, a lawn mower, and a snowblower. The puppy could barely move! There was a bowl of water by the door, but the puppy couldn't get to it.

Before Jack untangled the rope, he reached out a hand for the puppy to smell. "You can trust me, little pup," he said softly. "OK?"

Lizzie, Jack's older sister, knew everything about dogs. She had taught Jack that it was always sensible to be careful around a dog you didn't know. Especially when the owner wasn't around to tell you whether it was OK to pat the dog. Most dogs are friendly, but some aren't. And sometimes even a really nice dog will bite just because it is scared. Jack really wanted to help this dog, but first he had to make sure that it wouldn't hurt him.

The puppy raised his head to sniff Jack's hand. His long, floppy ears hung down, giving him a sad, hangdog look. He had a shiny little black nose and a sweet brown and white face with black markings. His legs and his round puppy belly were white, and his back was brown and black. He was almost as cute as Buddy had been at that age.

I think I like this boy. Maybe he'll pat me, if I let him know it's all right. I definitely could use a pat or two. I could use a hug. I could use a friend.

The puppy licked Jack's hand, and when Jack gave his head a pat in return, his little white and brown tail wagged so that it thumped against the garage wall.

"Aww, look! It's a beagle puppy!" By now, Sammy had joined Jack in the garage. He patted the puppy, too. "My uncle Jim has beagles. They are really clever. Now that I think of it, they howl like that sometimes just for fun."

"Something tells me this guy is not howling just for fun." Jack was busy untangling the rope. "Can you imagine being tied up out here all by yourself?" He pulled the rope free and gave the puppy a pat. "There you go, pal!"

Oh, yaaaaaay! Oh, hoooooray! It feels so good to move around again! I'm going to jump right up on this boy and lick his face. I'm sure he'll know that means "thank you!"

12

The boys laughed when the puppy pranced around howling, then put his paws on Jack's shoulders and licked his face all over. Then Jack and Sammy watched the puppy run over to his water bowl. After he lapped up every last drop, he sat down and looked at them, tilting his head expectantly as if he wanted more. Water dripped off his droopy ears, which had dangled into the bowl while he was drinking.

Jack picked up the bowl and took it over to a tap he'd noticed on the outside of the garage. After he filled it with water, he brought the bowl back to its place near a pile of dirty blankets. He guessed that was probably the puppy's bed. "Hey, look, there's a little sign here by his bowls. It says, 'Patches'. I guess that's his name." The sign was scrawled in red crayon.

"Patches!" Sammy tried calling. "Come here, boy!"

The puppy turned and galloped over to Sammy with his mouth wide open, his pink tongue lolling out, and his floppy ears flying. Now that the rope was untangled, he could run all over the garage and even out into the driveway.

Another new friend! Yaaayyy!

Patches howled with joy as he jumped right into Sammy's arms.

Sammy rolled over, laughing hysterically.

"Here, Patches!" Jack called. The puppy galloped back over and started licking his face. Jack cracked up. That made the puppy lick him even more. "Ha-ha! Stop!" yelled Jack. "You're tickling me!"

"*Shh!*" Sammy looked over at the house. "What if somebody's home?"

"Nobody's home," Jack said. "If they were, they would have heard him crying and let him in." He played some more with Patches, scratching him between the ears. Buddy always liked being scratched there. Patches seemed to like it, too.

"I would never tie Buddy up outside like this." Jack felt so sorry for the lonely little pup. "I think it's mean. Dogs like to be with people, not left alone all by themselves."

"Goldie and Rufus would *hate* being tied up," Sammy agreed.

"It's not fair. It should be against the law." Jack thought for a second. "Hey, maybe it *is* against the law!" he said. "Maybe we should tell somebody about this puppy. Somebody who could help him if his owners aren't treating him properly."

"Like who?" Sammy asked.

"Like Lizzie."

Chapter Three

Jack gave Patches one more pat and stood up. "It's Saturday, so Lizzie's volunteering at the animal shelter today. Let's go and talk to her." Sometimes Jack liked to do things on his own, without letting Lizzie get involved. His big sister could be *so* bossy. But he had to admit that she could sometimes be useful.

Sammy nodded. "Sounds good." He patted Patches, too. "Hang in there, little fella!"

"We'll be back soon," Jack promised. He checked to make sure that the rope was still untangled. He hated to leave Patches all alone, but if they could find help for him, it would be worth it. He kept looking back at the puppy as he and Sammy left the garage and cut across the driveway.

Poor Patches. He looked so sad!

Why are the boys leaving, just when they had all been having so much fun? Oh, boooooo! Come back sooooon!

Patches started howling again before the boys were even out of sight. "Ohhh!" said Sammy, putting his hands over his ears again. "That sound!"

Jack didn't like it, either. Hearing a dog cry like that made him sad, mad and upset. How could people be so mean?

Then he saw something that made him *really* upset. "Sammy, look!" he said. They were in the back garden of the haunted house now, but they could still see across the driveway to the house where Patches lived. Jack pointed to a big window on the side of the house.

"I don't believe it!" Sammy stared.

"Me neither!" Jack clenched his fists. He felt

angrier than ever. Why? Because somebody *was* home at Patches's house! A man was sitting there – just *sitting* there! – with his back to the window. He had white hair and he was wearing a red jumper, and he was calmly reading the newspaper. Since Jack hadn't heard a car pull up or any doors opening or closing, he knew the man had to have been there the whole time.

How *could* he? How could somebody just sit there and read the paper while his dog was crying his heart out?

For a second, Jack felt like marching right up to the front door of that house and knocking on it. When the man answered, he'd say – what? He couldn't quite imagine. That was when he realized it wasn't such a good idea. Jack was just a little kid. Why would this grown-up man listen to anything he had to say? The man might even get angry. He would probably say it was none of Jack's business how he treated his dog. And maybe it wasn't.

But maybe it was. Maybe somebody could do something about the terrible way that Patches was being treated. "Come on!" Jack said. "Let's get going." He ran for his bike, hopped on, and started pedalling. He could hear Patches wailing for a long, long time.

By the time they got to Caring Paws, the animal shelter where Lizzie volunteered every Saturday, Jack and Sammy were panting. It had been a long ride, with lots of hills. One hill was so steep that Jack almost decided to get off and walk, pushing his bike. But then he remembered Patches. He could practically see the puppy's sad face and hear his mournful howls. So Jack kept riding.

"I've never been here before," Sammy said as they got off their bikes in the shelter's car park. "I know they take care of dogs that need homes. And they must have lots of dogs right now!" They could hear barking echoing through the building.

"They have cats, too," Jack told him. "I think

19

they even take guinea pigs once in a while. But most people come here to adopt dogs or cats."

"Or to give them up, right?" Sammy asked. "I remember once a friend of my mum's had to give up her dog because she was allergic. She brought him to one of these places. They promised to find him a good home."

Jack felt a knot in his stomach. He hated to think about people giving up their dogs. He would *never* give up Buddy, no matter how sneezy or itchy he got! But he knew that bringing a dog to a shelter was the responsible thing to do if you really couldn't take care of it any more. It was a lot better than leaving it somewhere like a petrol station. That was where Snowball had been left. Snowball was one of the cutest puppies the Petersons had ever fostered. He was a fluffy white terrier who now lived a very happy and comfortable life with a lady named Mrs Peabody.

Jack led the way into the shelter. The barking

got louder as soon as they entered the reception. His sister was standing behind the counter.

"Hey!" Lizzie looked up and smiled. "What are you guys doing here?" She put down the pen she was using to make name tags for the dog cages. "Is everything OK?" Lizzie stopped smiling when she saw the serious looks on the boys' faces. "Jack, what is it? Is Buddy all right?"

"Buddy's fine," Jack said. "It's another dog that's in trouble."

"A beagle," Sammy added. "Just a little puppy."

Lizzie came out from behind the counter. "What are you talking about? What beagle puppy? Where?"

"He was all tangled up in his leash!"

"He was crying!"

"His name is Patches!"

"The people were *home*!"

Sammy and Jack were both talking at once.

21

Chapter Four

"All right, now. Tell me *exactly* what you saw." Ms Dobbins uncapped her pen. She was the director of Caring Paws, and she was *crazy* about animals. Jack sometimes thought Ms Dobbins liked dogs better than people. The director had told Lizzie to bring the boys right into her office when she heard about what they had seen. Now she wanted a full report.

Jack, Sammy and Lizzie sat across from Ms Dobbins. She had pulled a form out of a folder and she was ready to fill it in. "We keep track of things like this," she said. "If someone reports that an animal is being mistreated, we make a file for that animal and we follow up. If we discover that the animal needs our help, we get in touch with the police. In some cases, we even end up taking the animal away from its owners."

Jack was shocked. "Really? So if I didn't treat Buddy properly, you could take him away?"

Ms Dobbins smiled. "From what I hear from Lizzie, Buddy gets treated like a king. I don't think you have anything to worry about." Her smile disappeared. "But not every dog is so lucky. Tell me about this beagle you saw."

First she asked for the exact address of the house where Patches lived.

"It's on Ferndale Drive," Sammy told her. He looked at Sammy. "But we don't know the house number." He described the house and the garage.

"It's next door to the haunted house," Sammy added.

Ms Dobbins raised her eyebrows. "Haunted house?" Then she laughed. "Oh, I know exactly which house you mean. The old Turner place. It's been abandoned for years." She made a note on her form. "OK, now we know *where*. So, tell me *what*. What did you see?"

Jack and Sammy described the howling they'd heard, and how they thought it was a ghost, and how they had discovered Patches all tangled up in his leash.

Ms Dobbins kept nodding and saying, "I see", and "uh-huh", as she wrote everything down. Once in a while she shook her head and made a *tsk* sound. And she sighed when she heard about the man in the red jumper who was home the whole time.

When the boys finished their story, she sighed again. "I'm so sorry," she said. "I know how upsetting it is to see an animal being mistreated."

"So?" Lizzie asked. "What can we do?"

"Maybe our family can foster Patches." Jack had been thinking about that the whole time. Wouldn't it be great if Patches could come to stay with the Petersons? He wouldn't be lonely or bored at all. He and Buddy could play all day, and

25

then Patches could sleep in Jack's room, just like Buddy always did.

But Ms Dobbins was shaking her head. "I don't think so," she said. "We can't just swoop in and take Patches away from his family. Not unless they're doing something that's against the law, like hitting him."

"But—" Sammy began.

"Our laws make it hard to take a dog away," Ms. Dobbins went on. "If Patches has shelter, water and a lead that's at least four times as long as he is, then there's nothing we can do. If he has those things, he has the basic necessities."

Jack and Sammy looked at each other. Patches had all those things.

"But he couldn't *get* to his water, because he was tangled!" Jack said. "Plus it's just so *mean* to leave him alone out there!"

"It's not against the law for a dog to be lonely," Ms Dobbins said gently. "And the people probably aren't being unkind on purpose. Lots of people just don't understand that dogs need human companionship, playtime and love. That's part of our job here at the shelter – to teach people about how to be good pet owners."

"But how do you do that?" Jack asked.

"Sometimes we talk to the owners," Ms Dobbins told him. "But we also try to educate the public in general. We write newspaper articles and letters to the editor, and we sponsor special events."

"Remember when Meg Parker and Sergeant Frost and their dogs came to school to do that demonstration about dogs who help people?" Lizzie asked. "Ms Dobbins helped to set that up."

Ms Dobbins put down her pen. "I will drive by the house a few times and see how things look," she promised. "I imagine you'll keep an eye on Patches, too. If you see something happen that you think is really wrong, you can call me or just call the police. Don't try to talk to the owners yourselves, OK?"

Jack and Sammy nodded. "OK," they said together.

"I want to thank both of you for coming to me about this," Ms Dobbins said. "It's nice to know that there are people out there who really care about animals."

"A puppy like Patches needs somebody to stand up for him," said Jack. "He's too little to take care of himself."

"Well, I'm sure he's very happy to have found such good friends." Ms. Dobbins stood up and shook Jack's hand, then Sammy's.

Jack wasn't sure whether they had really done anything to help Patches. But at least they had tried.

CHapter Five

"So then Dagwood says, 'But, Blondie, I want to take a nap!'" It was Sunday morning, and Jack was reading the comics to Buddy, who lay on his lap. Jack *always* read the comics to Buddy on Sundays. It was their tradition. Snoopy was Buddy's favourite character, but he liked all the comics, not just Peanuts. The Bean was listening, too. He was curled up next to Jack, with his head on Jack's shoulder. The Bean loved Garfield best.

Dad and Lizzie were off doing some errands. But before he'd left, Dad had made blueberry pancakes for breakfast. Jack had eaten five, an all-time record. He was *stuffed*. Even Buddy had got a pancake – one that fell out of the pan when Dad was flipping it.

Mmmm, that pancake was so good. Buddy loved special treats like that. But the best treat of all was just being with Jack. Buddy loved the way Jack patted his ears while he read out loud. Maybe later they would go outside and play with a ball! Life was good.

"Jack!" Mum called. "Sammy is here!"

When Jack came into the kitchen, he found Sammy already sitting at the table, finishing off a pancake. Sammy almost always ate two break-fasts, one at home and one at the Petersons'. "Hey," he said when he saw Jack. "Ready to go and see Patches?"

"Who's Patches?" Mum asked as she put the syrup and butter away.

"Nobody," Jack said. "I mean, he's just a puppy we know."

"Jack!" His mother gave him a stern look. "Are you going to come home with another puppy to foster? Because if you are—"

"I'm not!" Jack said. "I promise. We're just visiting."

"OK." Mum didn't look totally convinced.

Jack didn't want to tell Mum all about Patches quite yet. He and Sammy had decided to spy on Patches's family that morning and make sure they were treating him properly. Somehow, Jack didn't think his mum would approve. Spying was not high on her list of OK things to do. But Jack thought it was important to check up on Patches.

Jack gave Buddy and the Bean goodbye hugs. Then he and Sammy hopped on their bikes and rode to Ferndale Drive. This time Jack walked right up onto the porch of the haunted house. Now that he knew all the moaning came from Patches, and not from a ghost, he felt safe.

"Here, behind these vines," Sammy whispered

when they got to the back porch. "We can see everything, but nobody can see us."

They sat down behind the vines. Jack pulled out the little notebook he had brought so that they could keep track of how Patches was being treated.

Patches was tied out in the garage again. But this time he wasn't crying. This time he was getting at least a *little* bit of attention. First, two kids came out of the house, a boy and a girl about Lizzie's age. The girl gave Patches a little pat when she passed him on her way to get her bike out of the garage. The boy didn't pat him, but he said, "Hey, Patches."

Jack could tell that Patches would have liked more attention. But the kids jumped on to their bikes and rode off. Jack made some notes in his notebook.

A few minutes later, a lady who must have been the kids' mum came outside. She went to the hose and filled up Patches's water bowl. His tail wagged when she put it down for him, but she didn't pat him or say anything to him.

"Wanda!" somebody yelled from inside. "Where are you?"

It must have been the dad. His voice was loud. Jack wondered if he was angry. Angry enough to be mean to a puppy? Jack hoped not.

"I'm out here with the dog," the woman called back. "I'll be right in." She rearranged the blankets that made up the puppy's bed, then headed inside.

Jack made some more notes while he and Sammy sat and waited for something else to happen. Nothing much did. After a while, the kids came back on their bicycles. They left them in the driveway and ran inside without saying hello to Patches. A little bit later, the whole family came out.

"Whoa," Jack whispered when he saw the dad. He was a big man, like rugby-player big. And he was frowning. He didn't even glance at Patches.

"Let's go," he said to the kids. "We're late."

33

The family piled into the car and drove off without saying goodbye to Patches. As the car disappeared down the driveway, Patches began to howl.

Jack didn't even stop to write any notes in his spy notebook. He jumped up and ran right across the driveway and into the garage. He gave Patches a big hug. "You poor guy," he muttered into the soft fur on the puppy's neck. "All you want is a little more attention."

It felt so good to be hugged! Patches snuggled into the boy's arms. He could have stayed there for ever.

"Jack!"

Jack looked up. Sammy was standing on the porch, waving both arms. "Jack, there's somebody home!" Sammy said in a loud whisper.

Oops! Jack gave Patches one last squeeze, then dashed back across the driveway. When he joined

Sammy on the porch, Sammy pointed to the side window of the house next door. The man in the red jumper was sitting there again!

"But that's not the only reason I called you back over here," Sammy said. "Listen." He held up one finger and tilted his head toward the front of the haunted house.

Jack tilted his head, too. What he heard made him gulp.

It was a low, moaning sound.

It wasn't Patches.

Maybe this time it really was a ghost!

Chapter Six

A ghost! Jack started thinking. What was the best way of slipping around to the front of the house so he could grab his bike and take off for home? But Sammy had other ideas.

He put a finger over his lips. "*Shhh.* It must be the ghost! Come on, we'll sneak up on it."

Jack wasn't even sure you *could* sneak up on a ghost, but he knew one thing: he didn't want to try. Was he scared? Not really. He just wasn't all that interested in ghosts. If Sammy was, well – fine! Sammy could sneak up on the ghost.

The moaning sound continued. Now Patches started to sing along.

Ohhhhh, where did you goooooo? Pleeeease, pleeease come back and play with meeeee!

Jack wondered if the new moaning they were hearing could possibly be coming from *another* lonely beagle in the neighbourhood. If so, maybe they could introduce Patches, and the dogs could become friends. No more loneliness. Problem solved.

While Jack was thinking, Sammy had tiptoed up onto the back porch. Jack could just get a glimpse of him between the vines. Sammy was inching his way over to a window, staying low so he could peek over the windowsill without being seen. Jack felt his heart pounding hard, as if *he* were the one up on that porch.

Then, suddenly, Sammy jumped back from the window and ran down the porch stairs. When he got back to Jack, his face was white.

"What is it? Is it a ghost?" Jack could tell something had frightened his friend.

Sammy shook his head. "No," he said, panting a little. "A lady. She's in there, painting the walls white."

"A lady? But – why is she moaning?" Jack was confused.

"She's not moaning. She's singing!" Sammy started to laugh. "Her back was to me, but I could see that she's wearing headphones and singing along. You know how that always sounds so weird?"

Jack did. Lizzie sometimes sang along while she was wearing her headphones. Dad said she sounded like a "lovesick moose".

"Anyway" – Sammy glanced over his shoulder, back at the house – "I bet she's going to come out after us. I think she heard me when I ran off the porch!"

Yikes. Maybe a ghost would have been safer.

Jack was about to suggest that they make a run for it when the back door of the haunted house slammed open. A young woman stepped out on to the porch. She was wearing white trousers and a white T-shirt, all splattered with different colours of paint. She was tall – and she looked *strong*.

"Noelle?" Sammy was staring at the woman.

"Sammy? Is that you?" The young woman stared back.

"I don't believe it," said Sammy.

"Me neither! I haven't seen you since Gram's birthday!" She was smiling now. "And I think you've grown two inches since then."

"What's going on?" Jack asked.

"That's my cousin!" Sammy pointed at the woman. "Noelle. She's *much* older than any of my other cousins. She's already finished college!"

Noelle laughed. "I'm not *that* old."

"This is Jack," Sammy said. "He lives next door to me."

"Hi, Jack!" Noelle smiled and waved. Then she looked back at Sammy. "So was that you looking in the window? Come on in, if you're curious. I'll give you a tour."

Sammy and Jack looked at each other. Jack knew he wasn't supposed to go into a stranger's house on his own – but he wasn't alone, and Noelle wasn't a stranger. She was Sammy's cousin!

A minute later, the boys were standing in the middle of an empty living room, looking at two big splotches of paint on the wall and agreeing with Noelle that "Historical Ivory" looked better than "Clamshell White".

"I'm a renovator," Noelle told the boys. "That means I find old houses like this and fix them up. Then I sell them to people who will appreciate them."

"Cool," said Jack. "But – didn't you hear that this house is haunted?"

Noelle laughed. "Sure I heard. They say that about *every* abandoned house. I'm used to it. And anyway, I don't believe in ghosts, so it doesn't scare me at all."

Jack liked that. He decided then and there that he didn't believe in ghosts, either.

"We *thought* there might be a ghost," Sammy said. "But the howling we heard turned out to be—"

"That adorable little beagle next door!" Noelle nodded. "I know. The poor little pup is so sad and lonely. I can't stand to hear him cry. That's why I was wearing my headphones."

All three of them went to the window and looked out at Patches, who had given up on howling for the moment. He was lying on the garage floor with his sad little face between his paws.

"His name is Patches. Can you believe the way those people treat him?" Jack asked. "They never give him any attention. But we found out that ignoring a dog isn't against the law."

Jack and Sammy explained about their visit to Ms Dobbins. "We're here to keep an eye out," Sammy told Noelle. "To make sure nothing really bad happens to Patches."

"That's a good idea," said Noelle. "I'll keep an eye out, too. I just wish there was something else we could do. I really feel sorry for the little pup."

Noelle showed the boys around the rest of the house. Jack liked the tall tower that you could get to by climbing up a ladder and through a trap-door on the third floor. Noelle said she thought it would make a great guest bedroom. She explained all about her plans for fixing things up. Jack had a feeling that, like Patches, Noelle was a little lonely. It must be hard to work all by yourself, day after day, in old, empty houses.

"Noelle is really nice," Jack said to Sammy as they were biking home.

"She's great," Sammy agreed. "I remember once she wrote a letter to the newspaper about this big tree we all used to climb, near Gram's house. The electric company was going to cut it down, but her letter made them think again. Now that tree is still there!"

That made Jack think. He felt so bad about

Patches, and – just like Noelle – he wished there was something he could do to help the lonely puppy. Now he remembered what Ms Dobbins had said about teaching people the right way to treat dogs. Maybe there *was* a way he could help.

When he got home, Jack took Buddy out in the back garden for a long play session. He and the puppy ran and tumbled and wrestled and played tug-of-war with a stuffed snake. The whole time Jack was thinking about Patches, and how much the little beagle puppy would have loved to play like that. The little beagle puppy would have *loved* it.

After dinner that night, Jack went straight upstairs to the computer and worked for a long time. It would not have taken quite so long except he kept getting interrupted. First by Buddy, who trotted in and put his paws on Jack's knee, hoping for more attention. Then by the Bean, who came in looking for Buddy. Then by Lizzie, who came in to scoop up the Bean for bath and

Chapter Seven

Dear Editor,

My name is Jack Peterson, age eight. I am a big dog lover. I don't mean I just love big dogs - I love <u>all</u> dogs. Even miniature poodles. That's why it makes me upset when I see a dog that is not getting the attention and love he deserves. Like this beagle puppy I know who is always tied up in a garage. He is so sad and lonely that he cries all day. Some people don't understand that dogs do not like to be tied up all day, all by themselves. Dogs like to be with people. They like to be played with and hugged. If you don't have time to make a dog feel like part of your family, maybe a dog is not the right pet for you. For more information, you can talk to Ms Dobbins at the Caring Paws Animal Shelter.

Hug your dog!

Jack Peterson

"What is *this*?" It was the next night, just before dinner time, and Lizzie was staring at the last page of the newspaper. "Is that what you were doing last night? You wrote a letter?"

Jack grabbed the paper from her. "It's in there already? Cool!"

Mum came over to see. She smiled when she saw the letter. "That's great, Jack. Your first published writing. Maybe you'll be a writer like me some day." Mum was a reporter for the same newspaper that Jack's letter was in. But Jack didn't think that was why his letter to the editor had been published. Jack had sent his letter in by email, just like it said to do in the paper. In the directions it said that the newspaper published just about every letter it received.

Then Mum read the letter. "Oh, dear! Where *is* this poor puppy?" she asked.

Jack and Lizzie told her about Patches.

"Well." Mum looked a little worried. "Don't get mixed up with the owners, OK? That's just asking for trouble. You should probably leave this in Ms Dobbins's hands from now on."

Fortunately, Mum did not make Jack and Lizzie promise to stay away from Patches. Jack knew he couldn't abandon Patches now.

That night, Jack read the letter over and over. It looked so official there in the paper! He read it out loud to the Bean and Buddy. Twice each, until Lizzie yelled at him to stop. Jack thought she was probably just jealous. When Dad got home, Jack read it to him, too.

"Nice work," said Dad. "Hug your dog. I like

that." He reached down and patted Buddy. Then he had to pat the Bean, too.

The next day at school, everybody was talking about Jack's letter. His teacher read it out loud to the class, but lots of kids had already seen it. "Hug your dog!" people kept saying to Jack when they passed him in the hall or saw him in the cafeteria or the playground. Even the head teacher said it. Everybody seemed to think Jack's letter was really good.

"You're famous!" said Sammy. It was after school, and they were biking over to the haunted house. (They still called it that, even though it wasn't really haunted.) They were going to check on Patches again, and this time, Lizzie was coming with them.

"I could have written that letter," Lizzie said.

"But you didn't," Jack pointed out. "I did."

Lizzie had no answer for that, so she changed the subject. "Is that the haunted house? Where's the puppy? I can hear him howling already."

"*Shh!*" Jack put his finger to his lips. "We'll

leave our bikes here. Then we have to see if anybody's home before we go see Patches."

Noelle's truck was not in the driveway. Jack and Sammy showed Lizzie where to lean her bike against the back porch of the haunted house. Then they climbed up on to the porch and peeked through the vines.

Patches was tied up, as usual. He sat with his head tipped back so his floppy ears hung down. They swung back and forth as he howled with all his might.

Oooohhhh, I'm soooo loooonely! Ooohhhh!

"Awww," said Lizzie.

"No car in the driveway," Sammy reported.

"No bikes in the garage," Jack added. "And if that old man is in the house, he never seems to come out, anyway. I guess the coast is clear."

All three of them dashed down the porch stairs and across the driveway. Patches jumped right up when he saw them. His little tail wagged so hard that his whole body seemed to wag. He licked Jack's face and Sammy's hand and Lizzie's toes. Then he tried to climb into Lizzie's lap, even though she was standing up!

Lizzie giggled. "He's adorable."

"He's clever, too," Jack told her. "I already taught him how to sit. Watch!" He turned to Patches. "Patches, sit!"

Hooraaay! hooooray! You came to playyyyy!

Instead of sitting, Patches spun around in a circle, howling joyfully.

"Well, we're working on it," said Jack, shrugging.

They played with Patches until they heard a car coming up the street. "Uh-oh! That might be the owners coming home!" Jack said. He quickly kissed Patches goodbye, and he, Sammy, and Lizzie ran back to get their bikes.

"Hey, you guys!" It turned out that it was

Noelle's truck they had heard. She was just unloading some cans of paint on to the porch. She pointed at Jack. "Hug your dog!" she said. "That was your letter, right?" She held out her hand for a high five. "Great job!"

"Thanks," said Jack. "This is my sister, Lizzie. She came to meet Patches."

"Isn't he the sweetest?" Noelle asked. She peered through the vines at Patches and shook her head. "I wish I could just untie him and have him keep me company while I work. I'd love to have a partner like him."

"Did Jack tell you that our family fosters puppies?" Lizzie asked. "Maybe some day we can find the perfect puppy for you, just like we did for your cousin Sammy."

"I'll keep my fingers crossed!" Noelle held up two twined fingers.

Jack thought he would keep *his* fingers crossed, too – in hopes that some day Patches's owners would give him the attention he deserved.

51

Chapter Eight

Sammy always said it was Jack's idea.

Jack always said it was Sammy's.

But they both agreed, when they talked about it later on, that it was probably a pretty *bad* idea. Even though everything worked out OK in the end.

The idea was this: Patches was so lonely. Maybe what he *really* needed was a doggy friend. And who was a better friend than Buddy? He got along with *all* dogs. And it was safe to let Buddy and Patches play together, because Jack knew Buddy had been to the vet recently and all his shots were up to date. That would protect him *and* Patches from passing around any bad germs. It was important to be careful about things like that with puppies. Jack had learned that from Lizzie.

"Hey, Buddy!" Jack said, the next afternoon. "What do you say? Want to go for a nice long walk?"

Buddy had been taking a nap under the kitchen table while Jack and Sammy ate cheese and crackers. Jack knew the puppy liked to nap there because sometimes he got to eat scraps of food that fell to the floor. Some fell accidentally – like a piece of Jack's hot dog at dinner last night. Some fell on purpose – like a few of Jack's string beans. But Buddy didn't care how the food got there. He gobbled up everything that came his way.

Now, when he heard the word "walk", Buddy jumped to his feet and scrambled out from under the table, knocking his head on the bottom of a chair.

Ouch! That hurt. But who cares? We're going for a walk! We're going for a walk!

We're going for a walk walk walk! Oh, boy! Oh, boy! Oh, boy!

Mom came into the kitchen just in time to see Buddy spinning around and barking while Jack tried to snap his lead on to his collar. She sighed and shook her head, but she was smiling. "You would think this puppy had never been outside before." She knelt down to give Buddy a pat. "Have a nice walk!"

Jack was glad she didn't ask where they were going. She had not actually *told* him not to go visit Patches. Maybe it was better not to give her the chance. For a second, Jack got a funny feeling in his stomach. Did that mean that maybe it *wasn't* such a good idea to take Buddy over there? But Buddy tugged on the lead, and Jack let the feeling go.

It took much longer to walk to Ferndale Drive than it did to bike there. Especially because

54

Buddy was in the kind of mood where he had to sniff every single blade of grass they passed.

Gee! Who's been here? That smells like Kirby, the big brown dog down the street. Or maybe it was Lucy, that cute little spotted one. No – I think it might be a squirrel! Yes! A squirrel!!! Or was it a cat? I'd better smell it again.

"Buddy! Come *on*!" Jack didn't mean to be impatient, and he hated to tug on Buddy's lead. He knew that Buddy really, *really* enjoyed sniffing things. But still, they were on a mission. Operation Make-a-Friend. So Jack tugged.

The haunted house was quiet. "I guess Noelle is working on one of her other houses today," said Jack as he and Sammy walked around to the back of the house.

Patches must have heard his voice, because he started howling right away.

55

It's yoouuuuu! Hooraaay! Come and plaaaaay!!

Buddy's ears went up.

Who's that? He sounds kind of sad!

Buddy pulled on his lead so hard that Jack had to trot to keep up with him. Buddy was small, but he was strong! He dragged Jack right across the neighbour's driveway before Jack could even check to see if anyone was home. Luckily, it seemed like everyone was away.

Buddy ran right up to Patches. The dogs sniffed each other's noses. Both their tails were wagging hard.

Hey! Hey! Hey! Stop that crying! I'll be your friend. Want to play?

Buddy stuck out his front paws and stretched his bum up in the air. His eyes seemed to sparkle with mischief as he invited Patches to play.

Whooooo are youuuuu?

Patches howled one last time. Then he seemed to decide that Buddy was OK. He stopped howling. He gave his whole body a shake, and his long ears went flying. Then he did a play-bow back at Buddy. A second later, the two puppies started to tear around the garage. And *two* seconds later, Patches's rope was *completely* tangled with Buddy's lead.

Jack and Sammy were laughing. The puppies were having so much fun together! It was great to see Patches so happy. He jumped up, put his paws on Buddy's neck, and pretended to bite him. Then he dashed away and let Buddy chase him. Then Buddy put his paws on Patches's neck and pretended to bite *him*. Then the two of them rolled and tumbled all over the floor, wrestling. The garage was full of puppy yips and growls.

"Go, Patches! Get him!" Sammy yelled.

"That's it, Buddy! Teach him a lesson!" Jack

knew the puppies were just playing. It was amazing how dogs could wrestle and snap at each other without anybody getting hurt. Their fighting was all in play.

Buddy jumped up when he heard his name. He cocked his head at Jack. Patches rolled over on his back and stared at Sammy, upside down. Then both puppies jumped on each other and the wrestling match started all over again.

"Hey! What's going on here?"

Jack whirled around.

His knees went weak and his stomach flipflopped.

It was the big man. The dad. Patches's owner.

Chapter Nine

"I said, what are you doing here?" The man was frowning. "And who's that dog? Why are you letting him fight with Patches?"

He stepped forward into the garage. He seemed bigger than ever as he gazed down at Jack and Sammy, who were sitting on the concrete floor.

Jack scrambled to his feet. "We – uh –" He could not think of a single thing to say.

"We were just playing with him." Sammy had jumped up, too. "That's Buddy. He belongs to Jack." He jerked a thumb at Jack.

The man squinted at Jack. "Your name's Jack?" he asked. "As in, Jack Peterson?"

Jack gasped. How did this man know his name?

"Well?"

Jack nodded. "I'm Jack Peterson," he admitted.

"The one who wrote the letter, right? Hug your dog?"

Jack groaned. So *that's* how he knew. Oh, man, was he in trouble now. He looked down at his shoes. "Yes, I wrote it."

Sammy took a step closer to Jack and faced the man. "There wasn't a *thing* wrong with that letter!" he said. "Everything Jack said was true!"

The man looked from Sammy to Jack. "Look," he said finally. "I want to talk to you, Jack Peterson. Why don't you and your friend and your dog come up on the porch?"

Jack would rather have come face-to-face with a ghost. But what could he do? He couldn't say no. So he tugged on Buddy's lead and called him over.

Hey! I was having fun! I thought you brought me over here to play!

"See you later, Patches," said Sammy as he untangled the beagle puppy's lead one more time.

Doooon't goooooo!

Patches started crying the minute they were out of sight.

The man led Jack and Sammy around the house and up onto the front porch. He gestured toward two chairs. "Sit," he said. Then he disappeared into the house.

Jack and Sammy sat down. They only had a second to exchange frightened glances before the man came back out, carrying a tray with three glasses of lemonade on it. He gave one to each of the boys, then sat down and took a sip from his own glass.

Buddy was sitting right next to Jack. He seemed to understand that this was no time to be fooling around.

After a moment, the man put down his glass. "So, you're Jack. And – what's your name?"

"Sammy." Sammy's eyes looked very big.

"Jack and Sammy. I'm Doug Stevens. And I guess you already know my dog, Patches."

Jack and Sammy nodded.

"Patches is a great puppy." Jack couldn't help himself. "He's really cute."

Then Mr Stevens did something that really surprised Jack.

He smiled.

"He sure is," he said. "I thought so the very first time I saw him. He was such a little guy, the runt of his litter."

"So was Buddy!" Jack couldn't believe it.

Buddy jumped up when he heard his name.

What? Are we going somewhere?

"You're joking!" said Mr Stevens. "He so looks healthy now." He chucked Buddy under the chin. "Hey there, little guy."

Jack couldn't believe it. Mr Stevens was turning out to be a nice person!

"Buddy is a lucky puppy," said Mr Stevens. "I can tell he gets lots of attention from you."

Jack wasn't sure what to say. "I'm lucky, too. I mean, lucky to have Buddy." He leaned down and gave Buddy a pat.

Mr Stevens didn't say anything for a little while. He just sat there looking at Buddy. Then he started talking again. "When I read your letter, I knew right away that it was about Patches," he began very quietly. "At first, I was a little angry. It was like you were saying I am a bad dog owner."

"I didn't mean—" Jack began, but Mr Stevens held up a hand.

"The truth is, when I thought about it, I *have* been a bad dog owner," he said. "Patches does not get the attention he deserves. My family is just too busy right now. We're all off on our separate activities all day, and there's nobody here to play with him."

"Nobody? What about the man who just sits there all the time, in the living room?" Sammy blurted out.

Mr Stevens raised an eyebrow. Jack could tell he didn't like the idea of Sammy and Jack looking through his windows.

"Not that we were spying or anything." Sammy was blushing.

"That man," said Mr Stevens, "happens to be my father. He's eighty-nine years old. He is in a wheelchair. And he's pretty much totally deaf. So he can't hear it when Patches is crying, and even if he could hear, there isn't much he could do about it."

"Oh." Sammy bit his lip. "Sorry."

"That's OK," said Mr Stevens. "I understand

that you boys only want what's best for Patches. So do I. That's why my wife and I have decided that this is not the right time for our family to have a dog. Your letter made us decide that we should find Patches another home."

Chapter Ten

Jack stared at Mr Stevens. "Really?" He couldn't believe that his letter had actually made Mr Stevens change his mind.

"You must think I'm a bad person," Mr Stevens said. "Somebody who doesn't treat his dog properly."

"No!" said Jack. "I mean – maybe I *did* think that, a little. But you just didn't *know*. It's just like Ms Dobbins said. She's the director of Caring Paws. You know, the animal shelter? She said lots of people just don't understand how much attention dogs really need."

Mr Stevens was nodding. "Exactly. My wife and I aren't really dog people at all. I got a puppy for my kids because I felt bad about them not getting to go away for spring break this year. I had to work, so we couldn't go to Florida like we usually do. But Hannah and Christopher didn't really *want* a dog. They're busy with friends and soccer and dance and all that."

Kids who don't want a dog? Jack had a hard time imagining that. He and Lizzie and the Bean had *always* wanted a dog. But as Dad always said, "Different people are different".

"My wife and I have already told the kids. They seemed to understand. So, I guess I'll give this Ms Dobbins a call," Mr Stevens was saying. "But I really don't want to leave the little guy at the animal shelter."

"It's the right thing to do," Sammy said. "They'll take good care of him there, and they'll find him a great home."

Jack was thinking. Maybe his family would end up fostering Patches. Wouldn't that be great? He and Buddy could play all day long! Jack reached down to scratch Buddy's head.

Suddenly, Mr Stevens cupped a hand over his ear. "What *is* that noise? I keep hearing this moaning sound. It's not Patches, it's something else. I always thought it was silly when people said the house next door was haunted. But lately I'm starting to wonder!"

Jack and Sammy looked at each other and started to laugh.

"It's Noelle," they said together.

"She's Sammy's cousin, and she's fixing up the house next door. She must be listening to her head-phones and singing along," Jack explained.

Then Jack and Sammy looked at each other again.

"Noelle!" they both shouted. Of course! Noelle thought Patches was cute. She hated to hear him cry. And most of all, she was lonely working by herself and wanted a pal.

Jack jumped to his feet.

"What is it?" Mr Stevens asked.

"I think we might know the perfect person to adopt Patches," said Jack. "Want to meet her?"

"Well, this is very sudden, but – OK." Mr Stevens got up. "Be right back, Pop!" he shouted into the house. Then he followed Jack and Sammy down the porch stairs, across the driveway, and up on to the porch of the haunted house. The ghostly sounds were even stronger now, but the boys weren't afraid at all.

Sammy looked through the window. "Yup, it's her!"

Jack knocked on the door.

There was no answer. Noelle was singing so loudly that she couldn't hear a thing. Jack knocked again. Then he gave up and pushed the door open.

"Hey!" Noelle beamed when she saw Jack and Sammy and Buddy. "This must be Buddy!" Jack had told her all about his puppy. She knelt down and held out her arms, and Buddy ran over to say

69

hello. Then Noelle saw Mr Stevens. "Oh," she said. "Hi." She stood up.

Mr Stevens walked right over to her and stuck out his hand. "I'm Doug Stevens, from next door," he said.

"Noelle Pagano," said Noelle, shaking his hand. "Good to meet you."

Mr Stevens looked around. "You're getting a lot done here," he said. "Nice work."

"Thanks!" Noelle crossed her arms. Jack could tell she was wondering why they were all there.

Mr Stevens could probably tell, too. "Listen," he said. "Maybe you've noticed our dog, Patches, out back."

"I sure have," said Noelle.

"I'm sorry for all the noise he's been making," Mr Stevens went on. "But, thanks to Jack's letter, we've finally worked out that our family is not really ready for a dog."

"Oh?" Now Noelle looked interested.

"So we're going to give him up for adoption."

Noelle was quiet for a moment. And for another moment. Finally, Jack couldn't stand one more second of suspense. "What do you think, Noelle? Want to adopt Patches?"

"Me?" Noelle looked surprised. "Well – I'd love to! But—"

"But *what*?" Sammy said.

"Well, a dog is a big responsibility," Noelle said. She looked thoughtful. "It's not something to rush into. But I've wanted a puppy for a long time and Patches would be great company. And my landlord already told me it was OK to have a dog in my apartment, and—"

"So it's OK!" Sammy said. "Come on! What are you waiting for?"

Sammy grabbed one of Noelle's hands and Jack grabbed the other. They pulled her over to the window so she could see across the driveway to where Patches was tied up in the garage. She looked at him for about one second.

71

Then she turned back to face Mr Stevens, and now she was smiling. "I'll take him. Definitely."

"Really?" asked Mr Stevens.

"Really!" said Noelle. "Should we go over and tell Patches right now?"

She led the way outside and across the driveway to the garage. "Hey, boy," she said softly as she knelt down to pat the puppy's long, droopy ears. "What do you say? Want to be my pal? Want to come home with me and keep me company when I'm working?"

Patches put his feet up onto Noelle's knees and licked her face. Then he plopped back down on to his little bum and pointed his face to the sky to howl a happy song.

Hoooorrraaaayyy! Hoooraayyy! Today is my lucky daaaaaaay!

Jack and Sammy grinned at each other and

slapped high fives. "You did it, man!" said Sammy. "You found a great home for Patches!"

Wow! Jack realized that Sammy was right. Even though Patches had never come to stay with the Petersons, he was a foster puppy just like all the others. Like Goldie and Snowball and Rascal, like Shadow and Buddy and Flash and Scout. And just like all the others, Patches had found the perfect for ever home.

Puppy Tips

What should you do if you see a dog (or any kind of animal) being mistreated? The best thing is to tell an adult: one of your parents, a teacher, or a friend. If there is RSPCA branch in your area, the people who work there can help.

If you love animals and care about how they are treated, you can do what Jack did and write a letter to the editor. Or you can do what Lizzie does and volunteer at your local animal shelter.

It's very sad that some people are not nice to animals. But you can make a difference by taking good care of your own pets. Don't forget: hug your dog!

Dear Reader,

Before Django, I had another dog named Junior. He was a black Lab, too. I adopted Junior from my local animal shelter when he was about one years old. He had been left at a petrol station (just like Snowball, in Puppy Place #2!). Junior was a wonderful dog, but it was easy to tell that he had not had a happy life before he came to live with me. He was shy and afraid of loud noises, and he hated it when people argued. He was the sweetest dog and very easy to love. Junior died of old age many years ago, and I still miss him!

Yours from the Puppy Place,
Ellen Miles

About the Author

Ellen Miles lives in Vermont, in the USA.

Ellen has always loved a good story. She also loves biking, skiing, and playing with her own dog, Django. Django is a black Lab who would rather eat a book than read one.